Ollie Outside

Screen-Free Fun

Michael Oberschneider, Psy.D.
Illustrated by Guy Wolek

free spirit
PUBLISHING®

Library of Congress Cataloging-in-Publication Data
Names: Oberschneider, Michael, author. | Wolek, Guy, illustrator.
Title: Ollie outside : screen-free fun / written by Michael Oberschneider, Psy.D. ; illustrated by Guy Wolek.
Description: Golden Valley : Free Spirit Publishing Inc., 2016.
Identifiers: LCCN 2016002907 | ISBN 9781631981050 (hard cover) | ISBN 1631981056 (hard cover) | ISBN 9781631980688 (soft cover) |
    ISBN 1631980688 (soft cover) | ISBN 9781631981081 (Web pdf) | ISBN 9781631981098 (epub)
Subjects: LCSH: Helping behavior—Juvenile literature.
Classification: LCC BF637.H4 .O24 2016 | DDC 649/.5—dc23
LC record available at http://lccn.loc.gov/2016002907

Free Spirit Publishing does not have control over or assume responsibility for author or third-party websites and their content.

Reading Level Grade 1; Interest Level Ages 4–8;
Fountas & Pinnell Guided Reading Level J

Cover and interior design by Emily Dyer
Edited by Elizabeth Verdick

10 9 8 7 6 5 4 3 2 1
Printed in China
R18860516

Free Spirit Publishing Inc.
6325 Sandburg Road, Suite 100
Minneapolis, MN 55427-3674
(612) 338-2068
help4kids@freespirit.com
www.freespirit.com

Free Spirit offers competitive pricing.
Contact edsales@freespirit.com for pricing information on multiple quantity purchases.

For the love of my life, Liz

"It's summer!" said Ollie.

His backyard had a big empty spot waiting to be filled . . .

and Ollie had a plan.

On Monday Ollie said, "Dad, will you build a fort with me?"

"I'd like to, but I have emails to send."

"Please?" asked Ollie.

"There's a big box in the garage. You can use it to make your fort."

Ollie moved the box outside.

He borrowed a welcome mat.

He made a flag.

Something was missing . . .

On Tuesday Ollie couldn't wait to get outside.

"Mom, will you visit me in my fort?"

"I'd love to, but I'm busy watching TV."

"*Please?*" asked Ollie.

"Not now."

"Well, can I use some of your gardening stuff for my fort?" he asked.

"Sure. Anything you need."

Ollie made a path with stones.

He dug in the dirt.

He planted flowers and watered them.

"Looks great!" he said.

But something was missing ...

On Wednesday Ollie decided to give his fort more color.

"Hey, Max!" he called to his brother. "Want to help me paint my fort?"

"No thanks, we're playing video games."

"Please?!" said Ollie. "Doing art is more fun."

No one answered.

Ollie painted the fort's walls.

He drew shingles on the roof.

He decorated the doors.

"Best fort ever!"

On Thursday Mom was online,
Dad was on the phone,
and Max was playing computer games.

Ollie found his sister and said, "Ava, come outside. I want to show you something awesome."

"Sorry, Ollie," she said. "I'm texting."

"PLEASE?" said Ollie.

"Maybe later," said Ava.

But she never
showed up.

On Friday the weather was so sunny Ollie wanted to spend all day outside playing fort.

He filled a basket with drinks and snacks.

"Who wants to have a picnic in my fort?" he asked his family.

Only Lucy followed him outside.

Ollie and Lucy played catch and fetch.

They smelled the flowers.

They watched the clouds drift by.

On Saturday the birds sang in the sun.
Ollie found some binoculars and went to see his grandparents.

"Hi, Gram and Gramps.
Want to sit by my new
fort and bird-watch?"

"We can't," said Gram.
"We're downloading photos."

Even his grandparents
were too busy for him!

Outside, Ollie scattered birdseed . . .

whistled to himself . . .

and waited for the birds to join him.

But something
was still missing ...

Ollie watched his family, thinking, "I should have named it **Fort Lonely**."

That evening Dad called out the door,
"Ollie, supper!"

Ollie didn't answer.

Mom called, "Get it while it's hot!"

Ollie hid in his fort.

He closed the doors of Fort Fun.

Ollie heard footsteps. And voices.

A furry nose poked in.

"Hi, Lucy," he said.

"What's wrong, Ollie? Don't you want dinner?"

"Awesome fort," said Ava.

"You did this by *yourself?*" said Max.

"You're right," said Mom.

"We were too busy with our electronics," said Dad.

Ava and Max told Ollie they were sorry.
Gram and Gramps gave him a hug.
Lucy licked Ollie's hand.

"I've got an idea," said Ollie.
"Let's all eat here tonight."

On Sunday that big backyard spot wasn't so empty.

Fort Fun was full.

"Finally!" said Ollie.
"Nothing is missing anymore."

Tips for Parents and Caregivers

We live in a technology-focused world, so our children are growing up with all kinds of electronics and media: TV and movies, smartphones, tablets, computers, video games, and apps (the list goes on and on). As parents and caregivers, we play an important role in modeling a healthy use of screens. Children learn from watching us, and then they practice what they see. Becoming your child's "screen-time guide" is a matter of knowing how to make the most of technology—and how much is too much.

Make face-to-face time the priority. Children thrive on interaction. They watch your facial expressions, listen to your words, ask you questions, and look to you for answers. A screen simply can't interact in the same way. This is why experts recommend limiting the amount of time spent in front of electronic devices.

Look for ways to stay interactive. Children *can* learn from educational technology, and there's plenty of it to choose from. But passive watching doesn't promote learning. If you're using screens, read and play along with your child, emphasizing interaction and focusing on the storyline. *(What happened there? Why do you think it happened? What might come next?)* Point to areas of interest, imitate the motions on the screen, pause to ask or answer questions, encourage lots of movement, and get up to take regular breaks together.

Supervise screen time. Experts agree that technology shouldn't serve as a babysitter or pacifier. Although it may seem convenient to set your child in front of the TV so you can get work done, children are better off playing with toys or "helping" you in some way (imitating your work or pitching in at whatever level they are capable of). Busy parents often find themselves handing over a smartphone or tablet to keep their children quiet or entertained in public places, but it's best to avoid doing this. Soon, a child may come to expect technology in the car or in the store. Remember, children learn about the world by accompanying you and watching what you do. Even "boring" errands are learning experiences!

Set up "screen-free zones" at home. For example, make it a rule that there's no screen use during snacktime or meals. Keep bedrooms screen free, too. Children who have free access to screens in their rooms tend to use technology more frequently. Studies have shown a link between screens in bedrooms and weight gain. And avoid the use of electronic devices before bedtime—not only for children but also for adults. Using screens in the evening and late at night makes it harder to settle down and fall asleep.

Focus on educational material. Children ages 5 and up have a wider variety of entertainment technology to choose from, and stronger opinions about what they like or don't like. But as the parent or caregiver, you still have the final say. Keep looking for high-quality material with a learning component. Remember that fast-paced content may have the effect of riling up your child. If you see this happening, step in.

Question the "norm." Today, more and more preschoolers have tablets and smartphones of their own. This suggests that electronic devices are becoming a regular part of the childhood experience. And yet, at what cost? Preschoolers and early elementary-school students are naturally curious about gadgets and media, but as a parent you ultimately get to decide what's right for your child. Children who sit in front of screens for long periods of time from a young age aren't getting fresh air, physical activity, and social interaction—all of which help them learn and grow. So be sure to make unplugged play the priority!

Schedule screen time so the limits are clear. The recommended daily guideline is no more than 1 to 2 hours total of screen time per day for children ages 2 and up. So, you might limit use of the TV to certain times of day or allow it only on weekends. Consider making the use of electronics conditional: "You can play the computer game for 20 minutes after you've finished homework and chores." Consistency is the key. Grandparents, sitters, and older siblings all need to know your screen-time expectations. Post the rules and set a timer to help everyone remember. Also, make sure the 1 to 2 hours of screen time reflect *all* electronic usage in a day. So, if you go see a movie together, try to turn off the screens and devices for the rest of the day.

Keep tabs on what's on. Place the TV or computer in a public area of your home so you can stay aware of what your child is watching and doing. Use passwords and parental-control features on electronics to block access to inappropriate material.

Limit your own use. Most of us could benefit from going on a "media diet" and becoming more aware of how much time we *really* spend in front of a screen. You may find it helpful to keep a written record of how much time you're on your phone, computer, or tablet and how often you watch television and movies. Your children are learning from your example. Make an effort to "turn it off": Avoid leaving the TV on in the background or channel-surfing while the kids play. Be sure to stay off the phone while driving. For conversations, shut down your device and talk to family members face-to-face. This isn't always easy, but it's important for your child's health and development.

Screen-Free Guidelines

* The American Academy of Pediatrics (AAP) says children under the age of 2 should avoid screen time. Studies show that the brain of a child age 2 or younger isn't developmentally able to process information from screens; young children may quickly become confused or overstimulated.

* Children over age 2 should be limited to 1 to 2 hours of screen time each day, with a focus on high-quality educational material. (Avoid media that's aggressive or overstimulating.)

* Always avoid violent content. Select age-appropriate material.

* Don't let your child use more than one electronic device at a time. This kind of multitasking isn't good for brain development.

Reconnecting...Without Screens

With a different approach to screen use, you may notice that you seem to have more time on your hands. Hours that once slipped away in front of the TV or computer now may be filled with more family time. Interaction is what it's all about: talking, playing, using your imagination, doing chores together, sitting down for a meal. Children benefit from these connections, and so do adults. In *Ollie Outside*, Ollie seeks such family interactions, but everyone is busy on their screens. Lost opportunities occur, but in the end, Ollie's family comes together and truly connects. Your family can do the same.

Experts know how important it is to keep kids moving—away from screens, on their feet, outside in the fresh air. According to the American Academy of Pediatrics, healthy child development depends on *unstructured creative play*. This type of free play—both indoors and out—gives children the chance to be active, build language and social skills, solve problems, and more. Make play a part of your child's life every single day.

Benefits of Being Active

☀ Playing outside helps children stay active and fit. The Centers for Disease Control (CDC) recommends that children do at least 60 minutes of physical activity daily.

☀ While it's important to be mindful of sun exposure, outdoor time increases children's vitamin D levels, which can help protect them from future heart disease, diabetes, bone problems, and other health issues.

☀ Children with ADHD or autism improve their concentration and focus after being or exercising outside.

☀ Active play promotes emotional development by relieving stress, increasing endorphin levels, and boosting mood.

☀ Time outside is linked to positive attitudes and kindness.

☀ Just 5 minutes of "green exercise" (exercising in nature) can improve mood and self-esteem—at any age.

About the Author and Illustrator

Michael Oberschneider, Psy.D., is a clinical psychologist and the founder and director of Ashburn Psychological and Psychiatric Services, a private mental-health practice located in Northern Virginia. He has been featured as a mental-health expert on CNN, *Good Morning America*, and other popular media outlets, and he has written articles for several news agencies, including *The Washington Post*. Dr. Oberschneider has also received *Washingtonian* Magazine's "Top Therapist" honor for his work with children and adolescents. He lives in Leesburg, Virginia, with his wife Liz and two children, Ava and Otto.

Guy Wolek grew up just outside Chicago. He drew constantly: on newspapers, inside the covers of books, wherever there was blank space. Today, some of his parents' books still have his art—so he can say his art has been in books since he was four! While growing up, Guy was focused on things other than art, until his first job after high school convinced him to attend the American Academy of Art in Chicago. Over his 35-year career, Guy has done everything from working as a courtroom sketch artist, to illustrating children's books, to developing characters for animation. He and his wife live in Southern California.

Other Great Books from Free Spirit

Zach Apologizes
by William Mulcahy, illustrated by Darren McKee
32 pp., color illust., HC, 8¼" x 8¼". Ages 5–8.

Zach Gets Frustrated
by William Mulcahy, illustrated by Darren McKee
32 pp., color illust., HC, 8¼" x 8¼". Ages 5–8.

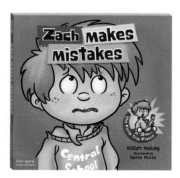

Zach Makes Mistakes
by William Mulcahy, illustrated by Darren McKee
32 pp., color illust., HC, 8¼" x 8¼". Ages 5–8.

Penelope Perfect
A Tale of Perfectionism Gone Wild
by Shannon Anderson, illustrated by Katie Kath
48 pp., color illust., PB and HC, 8" x 10". Ages 5–9.

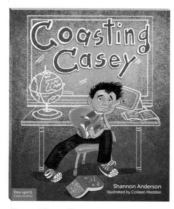

Coasting Casey
A Tale of Busting Boredom in School
by Shannon Anderson, illustrated by Colleen Madden
48 pp., color illust., PB and HC, 8" x 10". Ages 5–9.

Weird!
A Story About Dealing with Bullying in Schools
by Erin Frankel, illustrated by Paula Heaphy
48 pp., color illust., PB and HC, 9½" x 8". Ages 5–9.

Dare!
A Story About Standing Up to Bullying in Schools
by Erin Frankel, illustrated by Paula Heaphy
48 pp., color illust., PB and HC, 9½" x 8". Ages 5–9.

Tough!
A Story About How to Stop Bullying in Schools
by Erin Frankel, illustrated by Paula Heaphy
48 pp., color illust., PB and HC, 9½" x 8". Ages 5–9.

Nobody!
A Story About Overcoming Bullying in Schools
by Erin Frankel, illustrated by Paula Heaphy
48 pp., color illust., PB and HC, 8" x 10". Ages 5–9.

Interested in purchasing multiple quantities and receiving volume discounts?
Contact edsales@freespirit.com or call 1.800.735.7323 and ask for Education Sales.

Many Free Spirit authors are available for speaking engagements, workshops, and keynotes.
Contact speakers@freespirit.com or call 1.800.735.7323.

For pricing information, to place an order, or to request a free catalog, contact:

**Free Spirit Publishing Inc.
6325 Sandburg Road • Suite 100
Minneapolis, MN 55427-3674
toll-free 800.735.7323
local 612.338.2068
fax 612.337.5050
help4kids@freespirit.com
www.freespirit.com**